W9-COT-213

# My Day at the Baseball Game
## A Book About a Special Day
Heather Feldman

The Rosen Publishing Group's
PowerKids Press™
New York

1

For my loving Dad—for taking me to my first baseball game.

Published in 2000 by The Rosen Publishing Group, Inc.
29 East 21st Street, New York, NY 10010

Copyright © 2000 by The Rosen Publishing Group, Inc.

All rights reserved. No part of this book may be reproduced in any form without permission in writing from the publisher, except by a reviewer.

First Edition

Book design: Danielle Primiceri

Photo Credits:p. 6 © CORBIS/Joseph Sohm; ChromoSohm Inc.; p. 9 © CORBIS/Neal Preston; pp. 13, 21 © Rob Tringali Jr./SportsChrome USA; p. 17 © 1993 Brian Drake/SportsChrome USA.

Photo Illustrations by John Bentham

Feldman, Heather L.
       My day at the baseball game : a book about a special day / by Heather Feldman.
       p.   cm. — (My world)
       Includes index.
       Summary: A boy describes what happens when he and his dad go to a baseball game.
       ISBN 0-8239-5525-7
       1. Baseball—Juvenile literature.  2. Fathers and sons—Juvenile literature. [1. Baseball.]  I. Title.  II. Series: Feldman, Heather L. My world.
       GV867.5.F45  1998
       796.357—dc21
                                                                98-31954
                                                                     CIP
                                                                      AC

Manufactured in the United States of America

# Contents

My dad and I are going
to a baseball game.
I bring my glove to the
baseball game.

My dad and I eat hot
dogs at the baseball
game.

My dad and I watch the players run onto the field.

One team wears gray and blue. One team wears white and red. All baseball players wear sneakers called cleats.

A player called the pitcher starts the baseball game. He throws the first ball.
SWOOSH!

When a batter swings the bat and hits the ball we cheer, "HURRAY!"

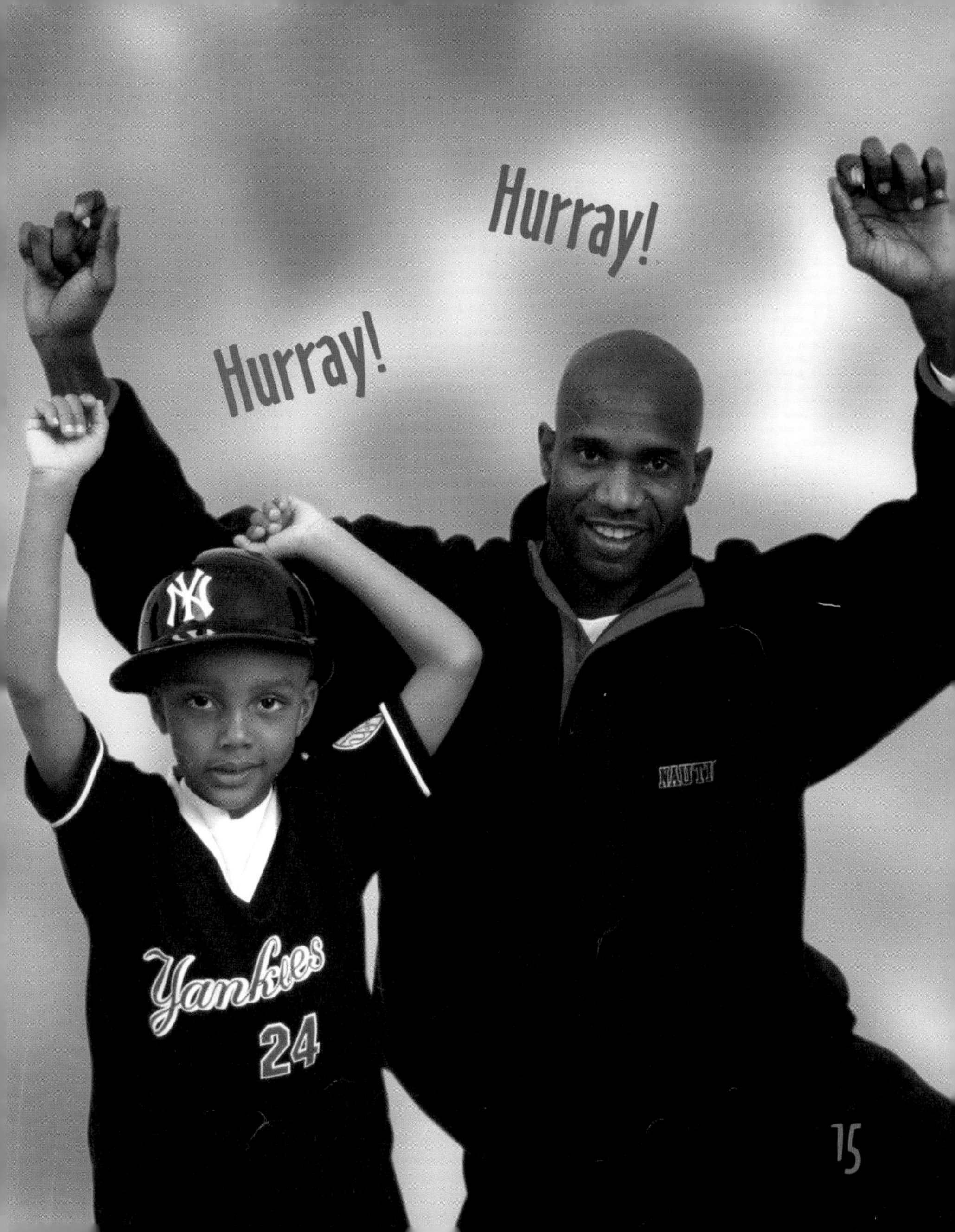


Hurray!

Hurray!

When a batter swings the bat and misses the ball, the umpire yells, "STRIKE!"

Strike!

10

17

Hurray!

My dad and I love when a batter hits a home run! We cheer again, "HURRAY!"

18

Hurray!

My dad and I have a great day at the baseball game!

# Words to Know
# A Picture Glossary

BASEBALL

BAT

GLOVE

CLEATS

UMPIRE

UNIFORMS

Here are more books to read about baseball:
*Baseball (A New True Book)*
by Ray Broekel
Children's Press

*This Is Baseball*
by Margaret Blackstone, illustrations by John O'Brian
Owlet Books

To learn more about baseball, check out these Web sites:
http://www.yahooligans.com/sports_and_rec reation/baseball/

http://www.littleleague.org/

# Index

Word Count: 125

## Note to Librarians, Teachers, and Parents

PowerKids Readers are specially designed to get emergent and beginning readers excited about learning to read. Simple stories and concepts are paired with photographs of real kids in real-life situations. Spirited characters and story lines that kids can relate to help readers respond to written language by linking meaning with their own everyday experiences. Sentences are short and simple, employing a basic vocabulary of sight words, as well as new words that describe familiar things and places. Large type, clean design, and photographs corresponding directly to the text all help children to decipher meaning. Features such as a picture glossary and an index help children get the most out of PowerKids Readers. Lists of related books and Web sites encourage kids to explore other sources and to continue the process of learning. With their engaging stories and vivid photo-illustrations, PowerKids Readers inspire children with the interest and confidence to return to these books again and again. It is this rich and rewarding experience of success with language that gives children the opportunity to develop a love of reading and learning that they will carry with them throughout their lives.